WEEKLY READER CHILDREN'S BOOK CLUB PRESENTS

Little Dog Lost

WEEKLY READER
CHILDREN'S BOOK CLUB

Little Dog Lost

by René Guillot

TRANSLATED BY JOAN SELBY-LOWNDES

Illustrated by Wallace Tripp

Lothrop, Lee & Shepard Co. ❋ *New York*

Also by René Guillot

THE WILD WHITE STALLION
THREE GIRLS AND A SECRET
FONABIO AND THE LION
THE STRANGER FROM THE SEA

✸ Contents

1 ❀ *Into the Woods*

*A*ll by himself. The red-brown Welsh corgi puppy ventured through the English countryside, into the heart of the woods in search of adventure. His short legs moved faster and faster as he raced gaily along the paths and bounded through the dense ferns, trying to catch a blackbird in flight.

Then, suddenly—*crash!* Before he could even yelp, the puppy was rolling over on the ground. He had been so busy chasing the blackbird. Now he was in trouble. A cat hiding in the branches of an oak tree had dropped onto his back. He fought as hard as he could, but he was held down, pinned under sharp claws. The spitting creature's paw reached dangerously close to the puppy's eyes! Just in time he was able to roll away. The little corgi, still trembling all over, retreated a safe distance away. The old gray tomcat sat licking his paw and seemed to forget that the puppy was there at all.

Using the inside of one paw, the puppy brushed off his muddy nose. Then, bright-eyed and eager, he set off once more, sniffing and listening near each tree.

For the rest of the day he played hide-and-seek with the birds and squirrels. He chased the wild rabbits, following them right to their burrows. All the different smells and sounds tempted the puppy as he wandered deeper and deeper into the woods.

The birds, roosting in the trees, had stopped singing. There was no sound, not a voice to be heard—only the deep sighing of the wind in the branches. The shadows deepened under the trees.

The puppy had raced about all day, and now he was alone and very tired. His coat was damp and matted, and his tongue hung limply from his open mouth. His little body trembled with fear as he collapsed onto the ground. How would he ever find the path home?

At this very moment his four little brothers at the farm where he had been born would be in the basket, lying snug and warm against their mother, Cora. They would go to sleep cuddled against her soft fur.

Cold, hungry, and lonely, the little corgi huddled with his nose between his paws, his eyes shut tight.

As the puppy lay there, his heart thumping, a long reddish-colored creature was creeping under the bushes, every footfall muffled by the moss.

It was a female fox. Creeping stealthily along, nose to the ground, the vixen was following a trail. She drew near, came around the trunk of the oak tree, and stopped.

The next moment the puppy felt warm breath on his damp coat. A strange animal was sniffing at him. He half opened his eyes and caught sight of two bright, gold-flecked eyes and the terrifying mouth of an animal baring its teeth.

More dead than alive, the puppy felt himself being hoisted

into the air. The big red-brown creature had picked him up exactly the same way Cora his mother used to do, taking him by the scruff of the neck and holding him carefully so as not to hurt him.

Gripped in her teeth, dangling from her muzzle like a parcel, bouncing and swinging, he was carried off through the dark woods.

2 ❧ A New Home

*T*he moon rose, full and round, climbing steadily in the sky over the wood.

During the whole journey, the puppy offered no resistance to the vixen. Once or twice she stopped to get her breath, putting him down on the grass and cautiously sitting as close to him as possible. Then on she went again, with the puppy in her mouth, till she reached a small valley with a stream running through it. Here, at the foot of the hills, dense thickets covered the rust-colored rocks.

The vixen was making her way to her den, hidden among the brambles in a cave at the end of a narrow passage. She crossed an open expanse of pebbles spread out at the foot of the rocks.

Two owls, perched in the lower branches of a tree, were on the lookout. Their luminous round eyes glowed red. Many times before the vixen had passed beneath their tree, and she had often carried one of her own cubs, dangling from her muzzle, held tightly by the scruff of its neck. But yesterday this had changed. Her cubs had been missing since the crows had flown back from the fields to roost. Shortly after the vixen had left her den and gone off to hunt, a wildcat came prowling through the brambles. It didn't take him long to find the en-

trance to the den. He slipped in between the boulders and devoured all of the vixen's cubs.

At dawn, when the mother fox came back to her den and found it empty, she was frantic. She raced through the woods, crisscrossing her own path, running in every direction. All day she searched the undergrowth, looking for her lost cubs.

It was nightfall when she found the tired puppy who had the same red-brown coat and pointed ears and muzzle as her own cubs. He was whimpering in the same tiny, high-pitched voice a fox cub has.

After smelling him she hesitated for a moment. In the end, though, she picked him up and carried him back to her den exactly the same as she would have taken one of her own cubs. She put him down on her cubs' empty bed of dried grass.

It was pitch-dark at the back of the cave. The puppy sat on the grass quite still, but alert and curious about his new surroundings. The vixen was lying stretched out beside him. She began to lick him from head to tail with big, strong sweeps of her rasping tongue.

This rough caress felt good to the forlorn little puppy. The vixen pushed him over with her paws toward her teats. They were full of milk, and the puppy was very hungry. Thrusting his nose into the coarse hair, he found a teat and began to suck. He went on sucking as though he could never be satisfied. His teeth were already coming through, and he was a good deal bigger than her lost cubs. He would need more than milk to feed on. But at last, fully fed, he curled up against the red-brown coat of this wild creature of the woods and fell asleep.

The vixen kept watch over her new "cub" all through the night. Just before dawn she slipped out of the den but only for a very short time.

When the puppy opened his eyes two fine eggs were set in the den near the vixen's forepaws. His new "mother" cracked the shells with her teeth, and watched contentedly as the puppy gulped the eggs down, then licked his chops. The vixen hovered over him and growled softly, a possessive look in her eyes.

Soon the puppy learned to reply with a bark whenever he heard the vixen growl. She would call him to come out of the den, and together they would set off through the woods. She was teaching him all the woodland secrets a fox needs to survive.

3 ❋ *Forest Secrets*

*N*ight was the time for going out.

Two weeks had now gone by since the mother fox had adopted the puppy. Already the young corgi was getting used to his new life.

The first thing he learned was to sleep in the daytime, as all foxes do.

The red fox was very gentle and patient with the puppy. Her low growl would be the signal. Perhaps the fox had spotted a cockchafer! Or a grasshopper! The puppy would then put his sights on the green insect jumping from leaf to leaf. In one bound he would catch it in midflight and crunch it in his teeth. But he was not yet fast enough to chase and catch a rat. That was the vixen's task.

He soon learned which trees could be climbed. It was no use trying the very straight trees. His short legs would reach only a little way around the trunk and his nails would not get a grip on the bark. He would heave himself up only to slide down again.

Often there were birds' nests in the fork of two low, crooked branches, and he could reach into them and find delicious blue or yellow eggs to crack between his teeth.

Sometimes the vixen's growl was sharp—a warning—perhaps a hedgehog, bristling with quills, was rolling itself up in their path.

Sometimes it was a reprimand—if a mouse within reach escaped the awkward puppy's lurch for him.

One night they came to the clearing where the rabbits had their warren. There was no sign of life near the burrows, though the round, full moon was high and bright.

The young corgi had been here before. Watching every move his fox-mother made, he copied her faithfully. She hunched over, her nose to the ground, following her own shadow. Little by little she raised her head. Suddenly she stopped and gazed up at the sky. Sitting on her haunches, motionless, she stared at the moon.

The puppy, crouching beside her, did the same. With his nose lifted to the sky, his neck stretched out, and his eyes bathed in the silvery light, he too "worshipped" the moon.

Then the hunt began. They went down to the bog, where frogs leaped among the rushes and the yellow-legged moorhens fled and dived as the vixen chased them. The moon was reflected in the still, mirrorlike surface of the water as if it had fallen in.

All the creatures who prowled in the undergrowth and overran the forest at night soon became familiar to the puppy. Wild boars came to wallow in the mud of the stagnant pools. Deer came out of the thickets to drink in the stream. The bleating

13

voices of the does could be heard calling their playful fawns. If they caught scent of the vixen, in a moment the whole herd gathered to run off and vanished like the wind.

The night's hunting finished at dawn, as the birds were awaking. The forest came alive with sounds of fluttering wings, the twittering of robins and hedge sparrows, and the cooing of pigeons. A magpie chattered to her brood.

Tap! Tap! Tap! A green woodpecker circled up the trunk of a tree, tapping the bark with his beak. In the leafy branches above him, a squirrel scampered back and forth, his plumed tail spread out like a fan. He dropped a nut from his high perch, hitting the puppy's nose.

That summer the vixen often led the corgi near the farm where he had been born. But he didn't recognize the house. It was true, of course, that he was not a fox, but he didn't know it. The memories of his early days had faded completely. He had forgotten his real mother Cora, the wicker basket, and his puppy brothers.

The puppy learned a fox's cunning was needed to get near that farm. It meant keeping well hidden before silently skirting around to the hen house. Then, wriggling silently under the wire netting, he could reach the perch in a single bound, seize a chicken, break its neck, and make off at full speed.

The corgi hadn't yet come across human beings or dogs in the forest, which was the foxes' territory. Now it wouldn't be long before he met them.

Autumn came, with strong winds tearing the leaves from the trees, and the English hunting season began.

One morning at daybreak there was a sound of gunfire in the wood. The corgi, trotting along behind the vixen, saw a hen pheasant fall out of the sky only a few paces from him. Almost at once there came the ferocious barking of a dog searching the undergrowth for the wounded bird.

The vixen's low growl warned the puppy of danger. He must run. But he couldn't. Frozen with fear, he remained rooted to the spot, staring at a huge animal that had just broken out of the undergrowth. It was the dog.

The hen pheasant had vanished under a pile of dead leaves, and the dog had lost her scent. But he had just caught wind of the vixen. With a threatening growl, he leaped forward to give chase.

The puppy could never have run fast enough to escape. With swift, brutal force, the vixen sank her teeth into the neck of the terrified puppy, picked him up, and plunged into the dense ferns.

It was a terrifying chase. They could hear the threatening bark of the hunting dog close behind. The vixen tried to throw him off the scent by doubling back on her tracks or by circling a tree to confuse the trail, but each time the dog managed to pick up the scent again and he was slowly gaining ground.

The puppy was a good weight, and the vixen, carrying the extra load in her mouth, wouldn't be able to keep up the pace for long.

She crossed the rabbit-warren clearing and made for a thicket. As she reached the edge of it, she swung her head around and, with a violent heave, threw the corgi into the air. He dropped like a stone into the brambles. Half stunned, he heard the sounds of the dog grow fainter. A few minutes later the hunter followed, calling him.

"Rambler! Rambler!"

The vixen had finally managed to shake off the dog at her heels by jumping into the stream and going with the current under cover of the reeds.

Making a wide detour through the forest, she came back to the brambles next to the clearing. Here she found the quivering puppy with his head hidden under his paws. He was still trembling with fear after his narrow escape.

From that day on, the vixen and her foster cub came back to their den well before dawn. There, safe in their bed at the back of the cave, they would hear the distant sound of hunting horns and the ground shaking under the thudding hooves of galloping horses. The forest seemed to echo to the sounds of a pack of hounds in full cry, but the puppy could sleep soundly, huddled against the red-brown fur of the vixen's flanks.

4 ❋ The Wildcat

*T*he little puppy spent all of his time with the vixen who had fed him with her own milk and watched over him so tenderly. To him she was now his real "mother," and the den was his home.

He learned from his fox mother that he was the young master of these big woods. Their hunting territory stretched through the whole forest, from the hills down to the bog. The pheasants, rabbits, and hares in this territory were theirs.

All these small furred and feathered creatures would go into hiding whenever the fox and her short-legged "cub" came by. Deer, does, and even the wild boar, fled before them.

To hunt a hare they had, first of all, to drive him out of the gardens or small meadows at the edge of the village. Their long-eared quarry preferred to be there, near a farm.

It was always the vixen who took on the task of driving him out, because of the danger to her "cub" of going so close to men's houses. With her nose in the air, she went the long way around under cover of the trees.

Meanwhile the puppy would make his way to the lookout

post on the hilltop. The path leading up to it had disappeared under the first snows of winter, but he knew that a running hare, with the vixen hard on its heels, would follow the path by instinct, for this was the path hunted hares always took to climb the slope.

Crouching low and ready to spring, the corgi watched the white expanse of the snow-covered plain below. Not for a second did he lose sight of the two dark shapes coming toward him. The smaller one was the hare; the bigger one, the vixen following close behind.

The bolting hare, his ears laid flat along his back, sped like an arrow. He was almost in range now. In a graceful arch the corgi sprang, seized the hare, and sank his teeth into the back of its neck, rolling over and over with it in the snow.

This was the way a real fox would behave. Yet there were still some traces of a dog's instincts left. The puppy didn't begin at once to tear his prey to pieces. Instead, he dragged it over to his "mother," bringing it to her in exactly the same way that a dog would bring something to his master.

This behavior always surprised the vixen. In fact, she was often faced with unusual reactions. This "cub" of hers, which didn't seem to grow, was different from others she had reared.

Although her "cub" was small and had short legs, he was old enough by this time to go hunting on his own. Why, then, didn't he try to go off by himself to scour the countryside and the woods? She would have to find a way to make him do it.

19

It was almost the end of December and it was snowing. The vixen had hesitated for a long time before deciding to put her "cub" to the test. Now the moment had come for him to go out and find food without her help.

The fox lingered, watching him sleep. Then, a bit reluctantly, she slid silently out of the den and plunged into the woods.

She hadn't gone far when the corgi awoke. He growled, grunted, and sleepily scratched behind an ear.

Suddenly he noticed that he was alone. His "mother's" place beside him was empty. He barked, softly at first, and then much louder. There was no reply.

Head down, he went into the passage leading to the lower level of their den. The cave here, opening onto the gallery, was also empty. In the ditch that served as a larder, where they always kept some game in reserve, the little corgi found only bits of fur and feathers. There was nothing to eat—not even a bone to gnaw.

Hunger was going to drive him out of the den. With drooping head he set off.

The vixen, making sure he wouldn't pick up her trail, had taken a track on which the snow had melted. A hundred yards from the den she had stopped and crammed herself into the hollow trunk of a dead tree. From this hiding place she could watch her "cub's" movements.

Off he went, sniffing the air, making straight for the rabbit warren. He had no idea that the vixen would be following him at a distance, under cover. She wanted to see how he would manage by himself, and watch over him without his knowing it.

He crossed the birch wood and came to the edge of the clearing. Then he stopped. What had he seen? Surely not a rabbit! There wasn't the smallest shadow moving on that still expanse of white.

The corgi had caught the scent of another animal, which also hunted in this part of the woods. It was a wildcat, and it was quite close to him, lying in wait, crouching under a snow-laden bush.

From a long way off the vixen recognized the lean shape of

her enemy. She was afraid for her "cub," who was going to meet this dangerous rival face to face.

A fight was inevitable, for the dog and cat were only a few paces from each other.

The corgi attacked first, but the yellow cat was on the alert, waiting for him. Rolling over on its back, all four feet in the air, the cat took the weight of the attack on its sharp claws.

A quick twist of its back, and the cat was on its feet again. It was the same size as the dog. They fought in a tangle of legs, attacking each other with vicious bites.

The dog was the stronger of the two, but the cat was more supple. Both of them instinctively knew that this was a fight to the death.

Locked in battle, they rolled in the snow. The dog was on top now, crushing his enemy under him. The wildcat fought fiercely, spitting and squealing with sounds that seemed to tear its throat.

The vixen watched from a distance, ready if she had to rush to the rescue.

Struggling in vain to wriggle free of the dog's grip, the cat squirmed like a worm cut by a spade. If it could strike with its claws and blind the dog by scratching out his eyes, it would easily win this fight. But it could not free itself from the dog and it was choking. There was a rattle in its throat. In a last desperate effort, it stiffened and tried to heave itself up and throw off the dog, whose teeth were already at its throat. But its strength was gone.

22

The corgi sank his teeth into his enemy's neck. It was all over.
Sitting down on the snow beside his dead opponent, the dog
licked his wounds. He had a torn ear, a scratched nose, and a
piece of skin hanging from one leg, but he had proved himself
in battle, and the vixen was reassured. She watched her "cub"
as he went off, limping slightly on his wounded leg. He was
ready to hunt on his own through the great forest and wide
territory of the foxes.

5 ❋ *The Fir Tree*

*A*fter his battle with the wildcat, the corgi again concentrated on his search for food. He started his night's hunting under a clear sky. Everything was strangely still and silent. There wasn't even the faintest flutter of wings in the branches or the smallest shadow moving on the ground. The whole forest seemed deserted. Hidden away in their holes or nests, the creatures of the foxes' hunting grounds gave no signs of life.

Even the rabbit warren was deserted. Only the snow-covered molehills were to be seen, lined up like a miniature mountain range.

Gradually, the clear night sky clouded over. The wind suddenly came up and blew in gusts, driving whirlwinds of thick snow on a mad chase through the trees.

It was impossible to find a path through this raging snowstorm. Running blind, the dog found shelter in an empty hut. Hours went by.

When the storm died down at last, the little corgi came out of the forest and made for the open fields. He ran the whole length of the great plain without finding a single trace of a hare. He climbed up into the hills. Sometimes there was food to be found up there, among the snow-covered fir trees: a bird,

with ice-encrusted feathers, its legs frozen stiff, might have fallen from a branch.

The night would soon be over, but the little corgi, exhausted, hungry, and chilled to the bone, had neither the courage nor the strength left to make his way back to the den. His throat was dry and burning, and he licked a snow-laden branch to quench his thirst. It was the lowest branch of a fir tree. He decided he could go no farther. Digging with all four paws, he

made a deep hole in the snow at the foot of the tree and crawled
into it. Here, huddled into a small ball, he fell asleep.

Daylight came, and a pale sun lit the plain. Two men were
climbing the hill to the pine wood. The taller of the two, wearing a lumber jacket and a fur hat pulled down over his ears,
was the owner of these fields and woods. His companion, who
carried a small axe, was the gamekeeper on this English estate.

"It's not worth climbing higher, Mr. John," said the gamekeeper. "Here's a good straight one. It'll make a fine Christmas
tree for your little Frances."

"Don't you think it's too big, Matthew?"

"Oh, no, Mr. John! By the time I've shaken off its coating of snow, I can easily carry it on my back."

"Go ahead then, Matthew, and cut it down. But be sure to take it off at ground level."

The gamekeeper went up to the tree. Crouching down, he began to clear away the snow that had piled up around its trunk. Then, suddenly, he called out. "Mr. John! Come and have a look at this! It's a young fox!"

At the bottom of the hole the corgi had dug for himself, only a ball of red-brown hair was visible. His head was hidden under his paws so that just the tip of a pointed nose was showing.

The corgi opened one eye. If he hadn't been so numb with cold, he would have attacked the faces leaning over him. But he was unable to move. All he could do was bare his teeth, threatening to bite.

"Take care, Mr. John!" warned the keeper. "Let me pick him up. I've got thick leather gloves."

Two heavy hands came down on the corgi, seized him, and held him tightly. He wriggled, beating the air with his paws. Half choking, he sank his teeth into a leather glove.

"He can't escape now, Mr. John. Look!" the keeper held him up. Then, amazed, he said, "But it's not a fox. It's a dog—a Welsh corgi! It must be a stray who's lost his master."

"It can't be, Matthew—not so far from the town."

"But where else could he come from? Only a dog who's lost would dig himself into the snow like this."

27

The dog, held prisoner in the keeper's hands, was now shivering with fear as much as with cold.

"Give me the little creature, Matthew," said John. "Look, the poor thing's got a torn ear and a scratched nose, as though he's been in a fight."

The corgi felt strong fingers stroking his rough coat, and rubbing him gently behind the ears. The voice that spoke to him was quiet and soothing.

"I know someone who's going to have a wonderful Christmas present tomorrow," the man was saying.

"Are you going to give him to your Frances?"

"Yes, Matthew! She's wanted a dog for a long time. Look! He'll just fit into my pocket."

He slipped the dog into the big pocket at the back of his lumber jacket, made for sportsmen to carry their game in. It was warm in there, and the corgi folded his paws under him once more and curled up very small. He hadn't yet had his fill of sleep, but he remained awake, alert to all the new smells and sounds the men had brought to him.

"Chop down the tree, and let's be on our way, Matthew!"

Matthew chopped down the fir tree and heaved it onto his shoulders. The next day would be Christmas, and John's daughter Frances would see the tree all lit up.

The two men made their way down to the plain. John's house was a long way off, on the outskirts of a big town whose church steeples were not even visible in the distance.

29

When they reached home, the men took the corgi into the kitchen, where they attended to the wounds he had received in his fight with the wildcat and gently brushed his matted coat. Then they gave him some warm soup and cut-up meat. Since he had been with the vixen, the corgi had only eaten raw meat. However, he gobbled down the warm, cooked food hungrily.

When he had finished eating, the corgi was placed in a wicker basket in a warm corner of the kitchen. The two men went out, closing the door behind them.

He couldn't understand being shut up in a basket. He tried to escape by forcing up the lid, but without success. Finally, tired of the struggle, he lay down.

For a time he listened to the sounds of the house. They were all strange and new to him—the purr of the refrigerator, the gurgle of a running tap, the ticking of a clock. Finally he fell asleep.

Sleeping at night was unusual for the corgi. He was accustomed to sleeping all day in the den with the vixen and waking only at dusk, when it was time to go out hunting. Today, for the first time, he didn't wake up at dusk. That was hardly surprising. The little dog had been brought in starving, exhausted, and half frozen. He needed time to build up his strength again. So he slept, not only all the rest of that day, but all night too.

Next to the kitchen, there was a big room with a carpet on

the floor, pictures on the walls, a gold-framed mirror, shelves filled with books, and a huge fireplace with a blazing log fire. Hanging from the mantelpiece was a row of stockings—big ones and little ones. Bright sunshine filtered through the lace window curtains and fell upon twinkling stars of every color, now adorning the green fir tree. Garlands and glittering glass balls hung from its branches.

It was in this room that the corgi woke up the next morning. He lay without moving in his basket, which had been placed at the foot of the Christmas tree.

Then, breaking the silence of Christmas morning, there was the sound of light footsteps running down the stairs and along the hall. The dog's ears pricked up as the door opened.

6 ❊ A New Friend

*I*t was nine-year-old Frances who opened the door and tip-toed into the living room. In the doorway she stopped, dazzled by the blaze of lights. Then, filled with wonder and delight, she ran to the lighted Christmas tree by the fireplace.

All the toys and presents were piled into the stockings and under the branches of the glittering fir tree. She could not remember a Christmas as beautiful as this one.

Kneeling by the hearth, Frances tugged at the ribbons and gold thread. There were boxes of chocolates and Christmas candy. And under the Christmas tree, close to a doll carriage, Frances found new toys. There were a doll with a complete wardrobe and a whole collection of games.

Looking through the cracks in his basket, the dog watched every move the little girl made. His heart was thumping with excitement and fear. Trying to escape, he started to scratch at the lid of his basket. Frances heard the sounds. She ran to the basket, which had so far gone unnoticed, and tugged at the fastenings. Then she pushed back the lid.

"Oh!" she gasped. "It's a dog! A real dog! I've always wanted one."

This was the best Christmas present of all. It wasn't just a

toy dog made of furry velvet, with glass eyes, but a real dog that could run around and bark.

"We're going to be friends," she said, holding out her hand to the cold, damp nose. Her voice was gay and musical, but the dog was frightened. When Frances tried to pick him up, he wriggled to get free. But despite his struggles, she finally lifted him out of the basket and held him tight against her.

"Your heart's beating so fast," said Frances. "Are you frightened?"

The corgi gave a low growl. He didn't like being held in the arms of this little girl. Only a few days before, he had been running free in the foxes' hunting grounds. He squirmed out of her arms and ran behind the tree.

Frances' parents, who had been watching quietly from the hall, came into the room. She ran to them and hugged them. "Oh, Mommy, Daddy! Thank you for the dog."

"What are you going to name him?" asked her father.

Frances thought awhile, then she decided. "I'll call him Tiny, because he has such short legs. Tiny!" she called. "Tiny! Come here!"

The dog, hiding behind the tree, hesitated a moment; then he dashed out, looked fearfully at the people, and scampered to the kitchen where he hid behind the stove. Frances ran after him. She tried to coax him out. Her mother cut up some meat, hoping that would help.

When Frances put the plate on the floor, Tiny ventured out from his hiding place. But he just took one look at the food and walked away.

"I know what it is, Tiny," Frances said. "You want to eat out of my hand."

The corgi came closer to sniff at the pieces of meat the girl held out to him. Then he made a little growling sound, snatched the meat out of her hand, and ran to a corner to eat.

"He took the meat. Oh, now I know we'll become friends. Mommy . . . can Tiny sleep in my room tonight?"

"Yes, but only on the condition that he's clean," her mother replied. "He must be bathed and brushed."

"You'll see, Mommy! He'll be sparkling." She kissed her

mother. Before Tiny could run, she picked him up and bounded upstairs.

The corgi splashed about in the bathtub, terrified as Frances soaped him all over and scrubbed his back and stomach. When he was dry, his coat was bright and soft. He leaped to the floor and ran to hide under a bed. He stayed there all day trembling.

But by dinner time Tiny had calmed down, and he came out from under the bed. He trotted down the stairs, came into the dining room where the family was eating, and flopped down under the table. Frances slipped pieces of chicken to him during dinner, and he gobbled them eagerly.

At bedtime Frances picked up Tiny and carried him upstairs to her room. There she put him beside her on the bed.

But he did not want to sleep there. Spread out on the floor was the skin of a wild animal with long fur. It was a fox pelt, complete with head and paws. Tiny thrust his nose into it. How well he knew that smell! He whimpered softly. At last he stretched out on the fur.

"Goodnight, Tiny!" A moment later Frances was asleep.

But the little dog—lost, bewildered, and far from familiar surroundings—lay awake for a long time.

After a while, it became easy for Tiny to live with humans. Frances was kind and gentle, and she loved to play with him. The garden had a wide, flat open space. Frances would throw a red ball as far as she could, and Tiny would run after it. He would bring it back to her held proudly between his teeth.

Going for a walk was not as much fun for Tiny. Frances would fasten a leather collar around his neck and attach a leash to it. And no matter how hard he rubbed his hind paw across the collar, it would not come off.

When they passed the hen house, the corgi would stop instinctively and stubbornly resist Frances' tugs at the leash. He would stand motionless in front of the wire netting, eyes alight, body quivering, and teeth bared, all the hunting instincts developed in the forest pulling him to his prey. Frances would scold him for his resistance, and Tiny would finally allow her to pull him away.

Over the high walls that surrounded the garden, it was just possible to see the tops of the trees. And in the far distance, half lost in the mist, were the hills with the pine woods, and beyond them the dark mass of the forest.

It was impossible to get over that wall to return to the forest. There was one place, however, where a dog might get through. A small garden gate, hidden at the back of some dense shrubbery, was often left ajar. But Tiny hadn't yet discovered it.

Often in the morning Frances dressed to go out but did not put the collar and leash on Tiny. Instead she would kiss him on the nose and say, "I'm going to school, Tiny. Be good."

Then Tiny would spend his day sleeping on the rug next to Frances' bed, until the crunch of pebbles near the front gate announced her return. If Frances picked up the red ball, Tiny would run with her to the garden ready for play.

One afternoon when he was chasing an especially long throw, Tiny came across the garden gate. The ball had rolled into the shrubbery, and the corgi searched for a long time before finding it behind a clump of trees right next to the gate. He sniffed curiously and pushed both forepaws against it. The rusty hinges creaked open, and beyond it Tiny saw the woods.

"Tiny! Tiny!" Frances was by the duck pond, calling him. He picked up the ball and ran back to her.

Frances stroked his head. "What are you dreaming about, Tiny?" she asked. "You look sad. You're not sick, are you? No, your nose isn't hot and dry! Don't you want to play anymore?"

They went back to the house together.

At dinner time that evening, when Frances called Tiny, he didn't come in. He hid in the shrubbery until dark. Then, slipping through the garden gate, he set off for the forest.

7 ❀ *Dog or Fox?*

*D*addy, will Tiny ever come back?" Frances was heart-broken. "He must know how much I love him."

"Of course he knows."

"Then why did he go away?"

A whole week had gone by, and Tiny hadn't returned.

One morning Matthew the gamekeeper came to the house.

"I have some news that will surprise you, Mr. John," he said. "You know the rabbit warren in the clearing?"

"You mean the one at the edge of the forest?"

"That's right! Well, what should I see up there but a fox—or, rather, a vixen—running through the snow. I've known that vixen for a long time. She's so cunning I've never been able to get her within range of my gun. I've even given her a name," he added with a laugh. "I call her Vickie."

"So you took a shot at her this time and missed?"

"No! I wouldn't have risked even taking aim, Mr. John," the keeper replied. "Listen to this! Just behind the vixen, following close in her tracks, I saw another creature—red-brown like a fox cub. The two of them reached the rabbit warren and then stopped and stood nose to nose, as if they were whispering to each other—like a pair of foxes do when they're hunting.

I watched them from a distance. Though my eyes aren't as good as they used to be, I had a clear view of the vixen lying in wait, crouching under a bush covered with hoarfrost. I couldn't see the younger one so well, for he was moving about, driving out the game for her. He went out of sight around the back of the warren. Then, suddenly, I saw him coming out again. He was hard on the heels of a hare that seemed to have been wounded, for it was losing ground. It would certainly be caught before it reached the bush where the vixen was hiding."

The gamekeeper paused and wiped his moustache with the back of his hand. "Of course, none of this is unusual," he went on. "But wait! After the creature had jumped onto the hare and broken its back, he dragged his prey over the snow and dropped it right under the vixen's nose. Then I saw—*he wasn't a fox!*"

"What do you mean, Matthew?"

"I saw with my own eyes," the keeper repeated. "It wasn't a fox; it was a dog—Tiny!"

"What?"

"There was no mistake—it was Tiny."

"Then that explains everything, Matthew!" exclaimed Frances' father. "Tiny is a creature of the woods. He's been brought up by that vixen whom you call Vickie. Sometimes a wild fox who has lost her cubs will adopt another animal. I must tell Frances as soon as she comes home from school. She won't have to cry over her lost dog anymore."

Three days after Matthew had seen the corgi hunting with

his fox mother in the rabbit warren, Frances came back from school to a big surprise. Tiny was crouching opposite the front door waiting for her.

Suddenly he jumped out. Frances, dropping her book bag, took the little corgi in her arms and hugged him. He licked her face over and over again.

"You've come back, Tiny!" she cried. "You've found your way home again. Mommy! Daddy! Look—Tiny's come back!"

"Frances, have you understood what your father has been telling you?" her mother asked some time later.

"Yes, Mommy. But Tiny isn't really a fox, is he?"

"No, he's a dog; only he learned how to survive in the forest. The fox taught him as if he were her own cub."

Frances thought this over. Then she said: "He must have come back because he's happy with us. So don't you think he'll learn, little by little, that he's a dog?"

"I'm sure he will." Her mother smiled. "But it'll take time."

"You mean he'll want to go off into the forest again?"

"I'm afraid so. You see, the fox who reared him has been a real mother to him, so he couldn't desert her, could he?"

"I suppose not," murmured Frances.

"We must make him feel that he's free," her mother went on. "The gate at the bottom of the garden must always be left open for him."

"I don't really mind," said Frances slowly. "I just want Tiny to be happy. I know he'll always come back in the end."

Tiny was really happy to be in the house again with Frances. At bedtime that night, he slept on the bed for the first time.

When Tiny disappeared for the second time, Frances didn't worry about him. He was gone for just a few days.

After that it became routine. Part of the time he was a dog, part of the time a fox. . . .

Each time he came back to the den, the vixen would greet him with little barks of pleasure and lick him all over to get rid of the smell of humans that clung to his coat.

When he left the forest and got back to the house, often covered with mud, Tiny had something else in store for him— a bathtub, soap, and a scrubbing brush!

41

8 ❈ *The Trap*

*O*ne spring morning Frances woke up with a funny feeling in her head and stomach. When she looked in the mirror, she was surprised to see red spots all over her face. When she pulled up her pajama top, she saw them all over her stomach too—measles! Frances had to stay in bed.

Tiny, crouching miserably at the foot of her bed, never left her room. He lost all his high spirits, his bright coat became dull, and he hardly touched the food they brought him. For more than two weeks he never went near the forest.

But as soon as Frances was well enough to go back to school again, Tiny's old urge to wander returned. That very morning he ran off to the forest.

"What are you thinking of, Frances?" her mother asked.

Frances was staring into the distance at the dark mass of the forest and the hills outlined against the blue sky. She turned toward her mother and smiled. "You'll be angry if I tell you," she said.

"Why should I?" said her mother.

"I was wishing—if only I could stay home from school today," Frances sighed, "and go find Tiny in the woods. I could hide in the bushes and see him meet his fox mother. I'd like to know

42

what they do together. Maybe he barks and then runs up and licks the fox's face, just the way he licks mine. Or maybe he doesn't act like a dog at all, but growls to her in fox language."

Her mother laughed softly. "I understand your curiosity. But you couldn't follow Tiny in the woods. A dog would travel too fast through the undergrowth. Now, off to school with you."

If Frances' wish had come true, at that moment she would have seen Tiny running merrily across the rabbit-warren clearing, then bounding gaily over the molehills and the clumps of pink heather.

As he came near the vixen's den he slowed to a jog, making his way down the rock-strewn valley overgrown with brambles.

The little corgi, creeping along the underground passage, was eagerly looking forward to surprising the vixen in her den. She'd wake with a start, and then, after rubbing noses, she'd sniff as usual at the collar around his neck.

The corgi squirmed into the den. It was empty, and the bed was cold. The vixen hadn't slept there.

The bewildered dog circled around the big cave, then scrambled down to the lower level and made his way back along the passage and out again into the wood.

How could he pick up the vixen's trail? Running zigzag, he sniffed the wind and cast about on the ground for a scent, but he failed to find the slightest trace of one.

Down by the bog he did come across some recent tracks in

the mud. The vixen had gone that way, but the trail disappeared again behind the clumps of reeds on the water's edge.

The dog ran till he had no breath left. He searched the thicket, crossed the open fields, and came back to the forest.

By now it was evening. Panting and tired, the corgi headed once more for the den. The vixen might have returned by this time.

He was following a track through a dense part of the wood when, suddenly, he heard a faint yelp. Tiny knew at once that it was his "mother's" voice. He stopped. His ears pointed straight up, and he held his head high, his tiredness all forgotten. He listened for a moment, to be sure of the right direction; then he raced through the undergrowth as fast as he could.

The muffled cries came from a clump of birch trees. He reached it, panting, and there he saw a terrible sight.

The red fox was stretched out on the ground, one leg caught in the iron teeth of a trap. Her fine coat was matted and caked with mud, and she lay on her side, exhausted by her struggles, scarcely able to move.

The corgi moved close to her. He heard her labored breathing and saw the blackened tongue lolling out of her mouth.

The vixen became aware of his presence and half opened her eyes. Her despairing cry was hardly more than a whisper.

Tiny raced back and forth, barking. Then he ran off into the woods toward Frances' house. After he had run for a short time, he heard the sound of voices in the depths of the wood.

44

They were human voices, growing fainter as they moved away.

Men were his friends, and he wasn't afraid of them. Instinctively he began to run after them. Taking a shortcut through the dense ferns, he reached the path and soon caught sight of a man and a boy.

"Look, Dad!" the boy cried out. "There's a fox behind us."

The man swung around and stared into the shadows.

A fox would have fled, but this strange-looking, red-brown animal stayed where he was.

45

"It's a dog, Patrick!" The man was astounded. "He must be lost in the woods. But what does he want with us?"

The dog was making little yelping barks. As the man and the boy moved toward him, he turned and trotted away, looking back at them over his shoulder. Then he stopped.

"He wants us to follow him," said the boy.

"You're right, Patrick!"

The dog set off again, making for the clump of birch trees. He stopped again, and let the man and the boy draw near. They were amazed when they saw the fox lying stretched out on the ground, with the whimpering dog circling around her.

"I can hardly believe it!" murmured the man. "This dog has made friends with a wild creature of the woods. Here, Patrick! Hold my binoculars."

The man crouched down to set the fox free, but first he had to protect himself from her sharp teeth and claws. Taking a piece of string from his pocket, he carefully muzzled her, then wound the string a couple of times around her legs and body. When she was safely tied up he released the trap. "Her leg's broken," he said.

"You'll be able to set it, won't you?" the boy asked anxiously.

"I'll do the best I can, Patrick. It depends on how much damage has been done. We'll have to get her back to the house. I'll lift her onto my shoulders."

The little procession set off along the path: the man carrying the wounded fox, the boy at his side, and after them, following a few paces behind, the corgi.

9 ✽ *Domino*

Patrick was ten years old, and he lived with his parents in a beautiful country home near a small English market town. His father was a veterinary surgeon, who took care of sick animals. Usually his patients were dogs, cats, horses, or other tame animals. Now, for the first time, he was going to treat a wild creature.

He took the fox into his office, which was next door to their house, and put her to sleep on the operating table under a brilliant battery of lights.

First he cleaned the wound; then he set the bones and bound the leg firmly with splints.

When Vickie, as John's gamekeeper had called her, woke up, she found herself on a bed of straw in a cage. She opened her eyes, and the first thing she saw was her foster cub, his nose pressed against the bars of the cage.

The vixen's growl was soft and friendly.

The corgi would have remained there, without moving or eating, if Patrick hadn't come to get him to take him back into the house.

Tiny had lost his collar during his frantic search for his "mother." Patrick had no way of knowing that Tiny belonged to Frances. He loved animals, and he wanted to adopt this little dog with the sad, questioning eyes.

"We can keep him, can't we, Dad?" he pleaded.

"I have no objection, Patrick," his father replied. "But will he want to stay?"

"He knows me already," Patrick told him. "He follows me around, and he comes when I call him."

"Oh, did you give him a name already?" His father smiled.

"I thought he wouldn't have one," Patrick began, "so I've named him Domino." Then he called to the dog: "Let's go and see how the fox is. Come on, Domino!"

The dog followed him across the courtyard to the hospital kennels, lined with cages for all the animals who were patients. There were dogs and cats, and even a parrot with an ear-splitting voice that never stopped talking and screeching at its neighbors.

The vixen, lying on the straw, got up the moment she saw the corgi. Through the bars of the cage, the dog and the fox licked each other's noses.

"You see, Domino? She'll soon be better, and then Dad will take off the bandages," Patrick told him. "She may be a bit lame, but she'll be able to run in the woods all right—when we set her free."

At the end of a week the vixen was almost well again. She began pacing restlessly round and round her cage.

One evening the veterinary surgeon left the door of her cage unlocked.

"Tonight she'll make her way back to the woods," he told Patrick.

She didn't go alone. Next morning the corgi's bed was empty too. He had left the house to follow his "mother" back to the forest.

During all this time, in another house, a very unhappy girl waited, hoping each day to see her dog come back.

"Tiny's been gone for more than two weeks now, Mommy," Frances said. "He's *never* been gone this long before."

She still had faith that he would come back.

When Tiny and the vixen had left the vet's house, they had headed straight for their territory. They had searched for food in their familiar woods and hunted in the fields and the rabbit clearing.

But after three days in the forest, the corgi became restless. Waiting till the vixen was asleep, he set off once more along the familiar path that led to Frances' house.

Frances found him on the doorstep when she left the house in the morning to go to school. That day, for the first time, he followed her and waited on the pavement outside the school gates. Then they went home together.

By the next day, Tiny had taken up his old habits of being a pet dog again.

Frances believed Tiny wouldn't go away again. But one morning she woke up to find that he wasn't lying by her bed.

50

A few days later he was back again, sheepishly willing to be bathed, scolded, hugged, and forgiven.

Next time he was away longer than usual, and Frances was beginning to worry about him again.

When Tiny did come back at last, however, she was astonished to see that he was wearing a brand new collar of red leather. She noticed another extraordinary thing, too. He wasn't caked with mud as usual. His coat was clean and shining, as if someone had been brushing him. These were mysteries that set everyone in the house guessing.

After his last visit to the foxes' wood, the corgi had retraced the path to Patrick's house.

When Domino appeared and jumped up to greet him, Patrick was filled with delight. He stayed two days with his new friend. Here, too, he slept in a room, lying by Patrick's bed.

When he set off for Frances' house again, the dog was wearing a red collar, which Patrick had bought him.

Frances quickly took the collar off.

"There are a lot of mysteries surrounding this little animal!" said her father.

"Come, Tiny," Frances called to him on Sunday. The little dog quivered all over with delight, and together they set out for a long walk. Going into the country with Frances was one of the things he loved best. This time they walked as far as the edge of the forest.

51

Suddenly a rider came in sight, cantering under the trees. It was a boy with red hair, wearing riding breeches and boots. Coming out into an open field, he set the pony at a fast gallop. From a distance they could see him crouching over its neck as he rode straight for a fence.

But instead of jumping the obstacle, the pony stopped dead and reared up. The boy was thrown, and he rolled over on the ground.

Frances cried out in alarm, and began running toward him.
He got up almost at once, however, and caught the pony before
it could escape.

Though Frances ran as fast as she could, Tiny raced ahead
of her. "Tiny!" she called. "Tiny!"

The dog came back, but he remained on the alert, his nose
in the air. Then, to her astonishment, Frances heard the boy
call out.

"Domino! Domino!"

53

The corgi shot away. He jumped up on the boy, licking his cheek in greeting.

"Tiny! Tiny!"

Frances walked up to the boy who was holding her dog. "Hello, my name is Frances."

"I'm Patrick. My dog. . . ."

"He's *my* dog," interrupted the little girl. "He's Tiny."

"No, he isn't Tiny," the boy insisted. "He's Domino!"

Frances told Patrick the whole story, beginning with the moment her father had found a cold, hungry dog buried in the snow at the foot of a fir tree. When she was finished, Patrick told her about a Welsh corgi that had led him and his father to the fox caught in a trap.

"That's Vickie," said Frances. "Matthew our gamekeeper calls her that."

"She seems to be Domino's foster mother," said the boy.

"Tiny's," she corrected him.

Tiny . . . Domino . . . the dog, hearing his two names, turned to look, first at Frances, then at Patrick. He plunked himself down between them.

"I have to go home. Would you please hand Domino up to me after I mount?" Patrick put his foot in a stirrup and swung expertly into the saddle. "Sometime I'll bring him to your house. Where do you live?"

Frances told him. Then she said, "I must get home, too! But I *won't* give you Tiny! He was mine first."

"Mine," yelled Patrick. "And I'll prove it to you. He'll follow his *real* owner, won't he? Well, let's give him that choice. We'll go off in opposite directions without calling him, and then we'll see which one of us he follows. And I'll bet it will be me."

Frances thought for awhile; then she agreed. Tiny just *had* to follow her. She knew he would.

The corgi didn't hesitate for a moment. He watched Patrick set his pony at a canter and go off. Then, turning, he followed Frances, skipping happily along at her heels.

10 ✾ *Patrick's Idea*

After their first meeting, Frances and Patrick became close friends. On Sundays, the boy would often come and spend the day at Frances' house, or she would be invited to his house in the country.

The boy would arrive on his bicycle to get her. Frances had a bicycle, too.

Take care on the road," her mother would say.

"Don't worry," the boy would reassure her. "She'll be all right with me."

Though he was only a year older than Frances, he seemed almost like a grown-up. She felt safe with him. When they set off down the hill in front of the house, he would freewheel beside her, keeping his hand on her shoulder to steady her. Going uphill, he would help by pushing.

Tiny would run along behind them, delighted to have his two friends together and to share their games.

Patrick was always full of ideas. They went fishing in the stream, shooting with bows and arrows, or riding across country on Patrick's pony. Frances, sitting gingerly on the pony's back, would clutch his mane with both hands as Patrick led him.

Patrick was afraid of nothing. He could climb like a squirrel to the very top of a poplar tree, and he could dive and swim like a fish.

"When I grow up I want to be a pilot or an astronaut," he told Frances. "I want to fly planes and spacecraft."

He loved making model planes. They would fly them in the field at the back of his house, and Tiny would go chasing after these curious-looking birds with paper wings, ready to pounce on them as they landed.

Then Patrick had yet another idea.

"Come and look at this, Frances!" he said one day. In the corner of a shed, the boy had been working for some time on the construction of a glider. It had a wingspan of about five feet, was made of balsa, and had a cockpit of chicken wire.

"When it's finished, it'll be big enough to carry a passenger," Patrick announced.

"Not you!" Frances whispered anxiously.

"No! And not you, either," the boy said, smiling. "By next Sunday, though, everything will be ready for its first flight." He didn't say anything more, but his smile was full of meaning.

Next Sunday! Frances would never forget that awful day. Patrick had made up his mind and wouldn't listen to anything she said. He made fun of her fears.

They climbed up a hill in the field. "I keep telling you Tiny will be all right," shouted Patrick above the wind. "He's going

for a short air trip, that's all. Anyway, he'll just land in the field, and he can't bounce out with the chicken-wire cockpit secured."

The corgi was always ready to take part in their games, so he crouched obediently under the cockpit as Patrick fastened it down.

"Here goes!" cried Patrick, holding the glider above him.

A gust of wind carried the glider away with a jerk. But Patrick hadn't reckoned on the dog's behavior. Tiny nervously jumped around the cockpit, setting the glider off-balance. Instead of landing smoothly, it crashed to the ground. Terrified, Tiny leaped from the cockpit which had bounced open. He bounded across the field into the forest without even looking back.

"Tiny! Tiny! Come back!" screamed Frances. But it was useless.

Patrick's face was a picture of guilt, but Frances was too upset to blame him.

11 ❊ The Secret of the Woodshed

*T*he little corgi raced through the forest, whimpering. Finally he tired, and crept into the undergrowth to hide. He lay there for some time, panting. At nightfall he came out of hiding. After the ride in the glider, he had had enough of people for a while. He would go to the vixen's den.

Late that night, he caught scent of her trail. He followed it to the familiar place in the forest where her den was. He squirmed into the den, and there he found his fox mother— lying down. She wasn't out hunting as usual this night.

The vixen was beginning to feel her age. When Tiny found her, she was weak with hunger. She could no longer run fast enough to overtake a hare. She was hindered by her wounded leg, which made her slightly lame.

So that night and every night for several weeks, Tiny went into the forest to hunt. The vixen would wait for him in the den, and he would bring her a rabbit or a bird to eat, or even some frogs.

One night the vixen left the den with Tiny. Crossing the open fields, the red fox no longer led the dog. Instead, she meekly followed him. They came to the first houses, and the corgi had to turn around and run back to her, barking to urge

her to go on. When they reached the garden gate, she lay down along the wall behind the shrubbery, unwilling to take another step. At last, though, after hesitating for a long time, she followed Tiny inside.

Tiny led her around the house, keeping close to the wall. He was making for the woodshed—a safe retreat where she could sleep in the corner, on a bed of straw.

That night Tiny didn't go up to Frances' room. He stayed with the vixen, lying beside her on the straw, hidden behind a big pile of logs and firewood.

The next day was Sunday. Patrick arrived on his bicycle at Frances' house. As he got off the bicycle, he noticed something moving near the woodshed.

"Arf! Arf!"

It was Tiny!

Patrick ran to the back door and knocked hard. "Frances! Frances! Come and look!"

"What is it, Patrick? What happened?"

"It's Tiny! He's come home!"

The two hurried to the woodshed. Tiny was elated to see them. Yet he seemed nervous about something. He ran to them and then to the woodshed door, back and forth.

"What's wrong, boy?" asked Patrick.

Tiny went to the woodshed door and whined. Patrick rushed over, followed by Frances. He opened the door. There he and Frances saw the vixen lying on the straw.

"Oh, Patrick!" exclaimed Frances. "It must be Tiny's fox mother, Vickie."

Unafraid, Patrick moved closer. "Yes, it's the same fox Dad and I rescued from the trap!"

Tiny barked excitedly, and the vixen quickly limped behind the woodpile to hide.

"Look, she's limping," said Patrick. "Why, I'll bet she can't hunt anymore, and that's why Tiny brought her here. Imagine that!"

And so the corgi and his fox mother lived together in the woodshed. Sometimes they would go off together to hunt in the forest. But later on they didn't do that so often. Because even-

tually Vickie let Frances and Patrick come close to her. She began to like the food they brought her. Sometimes she and Tiny ate a whole saucepanful.

Vickie and Tiny would prick up their ears whenever they heard the children's footsteps in the yard. As the boy and girl watched them together, the fox and the dog would make soft rumbling sounds to each other.

"Oh, Patrick," said Frances one Sunday. "Now I know that Tiny has everything he wants to make him happy."

Until the next winter, Frances helped Tiny care for the vixen. When the first snow had fallen, just two days before Christmas, they brought the vixen into the house to stay.

It was Tiny's second Christmas at Frances' house. Frances thought of it as his birthday, too. She did not really know when Tiny was born, so she decided the day he came to live with her was the right one to celebrate. Under the tree were beautiful new toys for Frances, but an especially delicious new bone was there for Vickie, and a bright new red ball . . . just for Tiny.